ANAHITA

ECHOES OF A MILLION DREAMS

JEGAN ULAGANATHAN

Dedicated to

My parents, My Brother, My Friends and My Colleagues

Contents

Preface

In a world where every life carries the weight of dreams, some souls are destined to etch their stories into the very fabric of existence. "**Anahita - Echoes of Million Dreams**" is a tale of such a soul—a child born under the ancient skies of the Himalayas, whose journey mirrors the resilience of rivers and the untamed spirit of the wilderness.

This is not merely the story of one life; it is an ode to the countless voices that shape us, the echoes of dreams we inherit and transform. Anahita's odyssey is a celebration of perseverance, the courage to carve one's path, and the ripples of change that emanate from every life touched by her grace.

As you traverse these pages, may you find reflections of your own dreams and the quiet whisper of the river that runs through us all—unwavering, relentless, and deeply human.

Prologue

In the ancient silence of the Himalayas, where the wind carried the secrets of sages and rivers sang lullabies older than time, a child entered the world beneath a sky draped in starlight. Her mother, Devi, lay on a straw mattress inside a mud-and-stone cottage nestled within a remote village, her breath syncing with the rhythm of the earth. As the child's first cry pierced the cold night air, it echoed through the valley like the birth of a new song—a melody that promised resilience.

The midwife, an elderly woman with hands like bark and eyes like embers, whispered, "She is blessed by the river."

Devi, soaked in sweat but smiling through tears, looked into her daughter's eyes—eyes the color of the Himalayan sky before a storm. "Anahita," she breathed. "Graceful river."

A deer emerged from the nearby forest just then, stepping into the moonlight, its gaze fixed on the hut as if bearing witness. It bowed its head before vanishing into the mist. The villagers would speak of it for years, calling it a sign, a prophecy. But for Devi, it was simply a mother's prayer answered.

What no one knew was that this child's journey would be no gentle stream—it would be a torrent carving mountains, reshaping landscapes, and leaving echoes in every soul she touched.

CHAPTER I

Whispers of the Himalayas

Nestled high in the cradle of the Himalayas, where snow-capped peaks stood like ancient guardians and clouds draped themselves lazily around mountaintops, lay the village of Sitang. It was the kind of place that seemed untouched by time—a mosaic of stone cottages, prayer flags fluttering in crisp alpine winds, and forest trails etched into memory by generations of feet. The air carried a silence not of emptiness, but of deep listening, as if the land itself was waiting for stories to be told.

In one such cottage, built from hand-hewn stones and crowned with a sloping roof of wooden shingles, Anahita was born.

The birth was difficult. Devi, the village healer and a woman of quiet strength, labored alone by the flickering light of a butter lamp. Outside, a silver crescent moon watched over the valley, casting an ethereal glow on pine-needled trails and snow-fed streams. When Anahita's first cry echoed through the mountain air, it startled even the owls into silence. The wind carried it far and wide, a cry not of fragility, but fierce, urgent life.

"Anahita," Devi whispered, tears tracing down her flushed cheeks. She held the infant close, her fingers tracing the baby's impossibly small features. "Graceful river. That is what you are."

The midwife, her eyes rheumy but still sharp, nodded slowly. "She has mountain fire in her lungs. And a soul like water. This one is meant for more than this valley."

In Sitang, babies were born often, but none had been welcomed with such awe. The next morning, a deer—rarely seen this close to human dwellings—stood at the edge of Devi's herb garden. It stared straight into the cottage, bowed its head once, and vanished into the trees. Villagers murmured of omens, of old mountain legends speaking of children born when the earth and sky aligned. But Devi said nothing. She only smiled and wrapped her daughter tighter in a shawl of yak wool, heart heavy with love and something else—an unspoken knowing.

The first five years of Anahita's life unfolded like a song. She toddled after her mother through winding forest paths, her laughter ringing like temple bells. She collected leaves with the seriousness of a scholar and spoke to flowers as if they could hear her—which, in Sitang, didn't seem strange at all. She had an uncanny patience for the silence of things: stones, rivers, trees. The villagers often said she listened better to the wind than to people.

But then came the fever.

It crept in silently, like a shadow at dusk. One day, Anahita was dancing barefoot across the dewy grass, her face flushed with the joy of chasing butterflies. The next, she lay still, drenched in sweat, her skin hot to the touch. Her tiny body writhed with chills. Devi's hands worked tirelessly—steeping herbs, mixing poultices, burning incense, chanting mantras that belonged to no written language but had lived in her lineage for centuries.

The villagers visited in hushed groups, leaving offerings outside the door—juniper leaves, beads, clay figures of protection. Inside, Devi refused to cry. Not out of strength, but defiance. "She is my river," she whispered to the flickering flame each night. "She will flow beyond this."

For twelve days, Anahita floated between worlds. And then—just as suddenly as it had arrived—the fever broke. Her eyes fluttered open, unfocused at first, then sharp with recognition. Her lips moved to call out for her mother, and Devi wept then, clutching her daughter to her chest with a cry that echoed with both pain and victory.

But the fever had left a mark. A long, pale scar now curved from her right brow to her cheek—like the trace of a falling star. It was not grotesque, merely noticeable. Yet in a village where beauty was measured in symmetry and untouched skin, the scar spoke too loudly. Some villagers looked away. Children stared too long. And Anahita, once fearless, grew quiet.

She avoided the mirror at first. Even her reflection in the still water of the stream made her pause. One evening, she asked softly, "Amma, why did the river hurt me?"

Devi paused, stirring a pot of nettle tea over a small fire. "It didn't hurt you, my child. It tested you."

"But... it left a mark," Anahita said, fingers grazing her cheek.

"Yes," Devi replied, sitting beside her. "Like the river leaves marks on stone. Does the stone complain? No, it shines. Because only something strong enough to withstand the current can carry such beauty."

That night, under a sky brimming with stars, Devi told her daughter the story of the Sacred Scar—a tale of a warrior who had fought a battle not with blades, but with truth, and had carried the scar of it proudly as proof he had lived, endured, and changed the world.

From that day on, Anahita didn't flinch from mirrors. She still walked the forests with her mother, still whispered to flowers. But now there was something else in her step—a quiet resolve. She began to listen more intently, not just to birds and wind, but to the soft, persistent whisper within herself. A whisper that said her story was only beginning.

CHAPTER II

Seeds of Curiosity

The seasons in Sitang danced in slow, deliberate rhythm. Spring painted the hillsides with wild rhododendrons and soft crocuses, while summer turned the forests into a cathedral of green, sunlight filtering through leaves like stained glass. Autumn brought gold and fire to the trees, and winter wrapped the village in a hush of snow and silence. Anahita moved through these seasons like a spirit of the land, each one imprinting itself upon her.

By the time she was nine, she knew the mountain trails better than most adults. She could identify dozens of plants by leaf and scent, knew which roots cured fever and which berries must never be touched. Devi taught her not just the names, but the songs of the plants—songs whispered by her mother's mother, and hers before that. Knowledge passed down not by books, but breath.

They would walk for hours, Devi's shawl rustling beside her, a woven basket on her back. "Every plant has a story," Devi would say. "You must listen long enough to hear it."

And Anahita did.

She listened when the earth was dry and cracked, when the trees trembled before a storm. She listened to the river as it shifted paths during spring thaw, carving new curves into its banks. Her world was small, yet infinite in its layers. A single grove held more wonder than a thousand cities could offer—or so she thought.

But that certainty began to shift the year a group of travelers arrived. They were researchers from the capital, young men and women with strange clothes, sleek gadgets, and wide-eyed awe for the simplicity around them. They carried machines that beeped and blinked, and spoke in fast syllables that sometimes Anahita struggled to follow. They stayed for a week, studying medicinal plants, photographing stone carvings, taking notes under trees that Anahita considered old friends.

She was fascinated and wary all at once. One afternoon, she approached a woman named Meera who was typing rapidly into a small device. "What are you doing?" Anahita asked.

Meera looked up, surprised. "Logging data. Recording what we found."

"Why?"

"So others can learn. So we can share this knowledge with the world."

Anahita frowned. "Why not remember it? Like my amma does."

Meera smiled kindly. "Because memory fades. But data doesn't."

Anahita didn't respond then, but the words settled in her like seeds. That night, she asked Devi, "Why do people from the outside want to take our stories?"

Devi placed a hand on her daughter's head. "Some take. Others come to understand. You must learn the difference."

Still, curiosity began to bloom. The idea that beyond these mountains lay cities where light came not from lamps but from wires, where books filled giant buildings and ideas flew across invisible lines, stirred something in Anahita. She began to imagine herself in those places—not to abandon the forest, but to carry it with her into rooms that had never known its scent.

In the evenings, by the fire, Devi noticed her daughter's gaze lingering on the map stitched into the old tapestry that hung on their wall. "Do you dream of going?" she asked one night.

Anahita hesitated. "Sometimes."

Devi nodded slowly. "The river must flow. Even when it leaves the mountain, it does not forget where it began."

That winter, the snow came late, and with it, a sense of urgency. Anahita began to ask more questions. She pored over the worn books the travelers had left behind, sounding out foreign words and memorizing pages by candlelight. She built tiny models of water mills from sticks and thread, testing how the current could be turned into energy. When she wasn't walking the trails, she was sketching designs in the dirt or in the margins of her books.

The villagers watched with a mixture of pride and concern. "She is not like the others," some whispered. "She sees too far."

"She sees just enough," Devi would reply.

But even Devi could sense the pull growing stronger. One morning, while Anahita was collecting snowmelt in a jug, Devi came to her with a small pouch. Inside was a seed—a rare blossom that grew only once every decade, on a cliff edge no one dared to climb.

"Why are you giving me this?" Anahita asked.

Devi looked into her eyes. "Because you're not just growing up—you're growing away. And I want you to remember what resilience looks like."

Anahita cupped the seed in her hand. It was no bigger than a fingernail, but it felt heavy with meaning.

Over the next weeks, she began to prepare for the idea of leaving—not with fear, but with quiet purpose. She spoke to the river each morning. She sat with her back against the oldest tree in the forest and closed her eyes until she could feel its roots beneath her own skin. She made promises—to her home, to the earth, to herself.

On the eve of her sixteenth birthday, as snowflakes began to fall like feathers from the darkening sky, Anahita stood at the edge of the village and whispered into the wind, "I will carry you with me."

The mountains did not answer, but something in her heart stirred in reply. It was the sound of a door opening—a future unfolding.

CHAPTER III

A Leap of Faith

The day Anahita announced her decision to leave Sitang, the air seemed to shift. The wind, which had always felt like a lullaby, turned sharper—more watchful. As if the mountains themselves were listening.

It happened one quiet morning after the snow had begun to melt, revealing dark patches of earth and the stubborn green of new shoots. Anahita sat with Devi near the river, their hands busy weaving a new mat from reeds. They had done this hundreds of times before, but this morning, something was different. Anahita's hands trembled slightly, her thoughts swirling like the current beside them.

"I want to go to the city," she said, softly but clearly, without looking up.

Devi's fingers stilled. For a moment, neither of them moved. The river gurgled, uncaring of the weight hanging between mother and daughter.

"You've been thinking about this for a long time," Devi finally said.

Anahita nodded. "Since the researchers came. Since I saw how much I didn't know. I want to learn. I want to do something... real."

Devi let out a breath that had been waiting for weeks. "You've always looked beyond these mountains, Anu. I knew the time would come."

Anahita's eyes flicked up. "Are you... angry?"

Devi smiled, but it was a sad smile. "No. Just... remembering. I once dreamed of leaving too, you know. But life chose otherwise for me. You, though—you were born reaching forward."

That night, they sat by the fire for hours, talking about the city. Devi described it not as a mother warning her child, but as a woman painting a landscape she had only seen in glimpses—through visitors' stories, distant memories, and newspaper clippings. Tall buildings, constant noise, people who walked fast and didn't look up. But also: libraries as large as temples, universities that hummed with ideas, and places where dreams, if persistent enough, could bloom in the cracks between concrete.

The decision was made, but the village had to be told.

When Anahita shared the news, some responded with admiration, others with hesitation. "She's too gentle for the city," said one elder. "Too wild," said another. But most, despite their doubts, came forward with quiet support. They had watched her grow from a sickly child into a spirited young woman who spoke with the trees and mended bird wings with silken care.

On the morning of her departure, Sitang rose early.

Snow still clung to the edges of the paths, but villagers lined the trail from her cottage to the edge of the forest. Each person offered something—gifts small but heavy with meaning. A wooden comb, carved by a friend. A jar of river stones, chosen by children who had played at her side. A thick shawl dyed with forest berries, its scent a reminder of home.

Devi stepped forward last, holding a small amulet on a leather string. Within the glass was the rare seed—the same one she had given Anahita months ago. It had not been planted. It had been kept, protected.

"Wear this," Devi said, fastening it around her daughter's neck. "Let it remind you that your roots are here. You don't need to see the mountain to know it holds you."

Anahita held her mother fiercely. Neither spoke of goodbye. The word felt too final. Instead, they whispered blessings—one old, one new.

With a final glance at her home, Anahita turned toward the winding path that would take her out of the valley and into a world she had only imagined. Her heart thudded in her chest—not from fear, but from something brighter, something electric. The future was no longer a thought—it was a journey under her feet.

The trail was steep, lined with jagged stones and thin branches clawing at her clothes. Her legs ached. Her boots were too small. But she did not stop. At a cliff bend, she paused to catch her breath and looked back. Sitang shimmered below, tucked in like a dream beneath clouds and snow.

She touched the amulet at her neck.

"I'll make you proud," she whispered to the wind, not knowing if it was a promise to her mother, her village, or the land itself.

Then she turned back toward the horizon, where the mountain road bent into mist—and where, just beyond, the city waited.

CHAPTER IV

Concrete Jungle

Nothing in Anahita's memory—no story, no dream, no image stitched into tapestry or told by firelight—had prepared her for the city.

It was not just the size that overwhelmed her. It was the speed. Everything moved, all the time. Cars roared past like beasts made of metal and light. People streamed across streets in rivers of motion, heads down, eyes glued to tiny glowing rectangles. Noise pressed in from all sides—horns blaring, vendors shouting, announcements echoing from towering digital boards. And the smell—an odd concoction of exhaust fumes, roasting meat, stale water, and hot pavement—clung to her skin like a second layer.

Anahita stood outside the train station gripping the straps of her canvas bag, the seed amulet resting over her heart. Her shawl, a deep red against the dull grays of the city, fluttered uselessly in the wind stirred by buses and taxis. For the first time in her life, she felt small—smaller than the trees of Sitang, smaller than the shadows cast by the skyscrapers that reached up like fingers trying to grasp the sky.

She made her way to the university hostel using hand-drawn directions Devi had carefully helped her write down. Every turn felt like a test. Her feet moved forward, but her eyes clung to everything—neon signs, cracked sidewalks, children playing in alleyways, trees locked in concrete squares. By the time she reached her dormitory, her body was sore, her heart racing.

The room was small, just a narrow cot by a desk, with peeling walls and a window that opened to the brick side of another building. The bed creaked when she sat. She placed the seed amulet on the windowsill and stared out at the flickering city lights.

That first night, she cried—not loudly, but with the quiet shudder of someone who had tried to be brave for too long.

The next morning, she wore her best kurta and tied her hair in a neat braid, the way Devi had taught her. She walked to the university campus with a notebook in one hand, a tattered book on ecology in the other. The university gates loomed like a fortress. Beyond them lay crowds of students—confident, loud, laughing, dressed in sharp clothes and speaking in slang she barely understood.

In her first class, she sat near the back. The professor, a stern woman with steel-rimmed glasses, moved quickly through the syllabus. Anahita struggled to keep up. Words like "carbon credits" and "geospatial analysis" swirled around her. Her notes were a mess of half-formed thoughts and confused doodles.

After class, a girl nearby whispered to her friend, glancing at Anahita, "She looks like a relic from a forest."

Anahita heard it. She didn't let herself flinch.

Days turned into weeks. She lived frugally, surviving on cheap meals and sleeping in the chill of her thin blanket. She studied late into the night in the library, copying textbooks by hand because she couldn't afford them. Her scar, which had been part of her identity in Sitang, now became the first thing people noticed. Some asked how she got it. Others assumed it was from an accident. A few simply stared, then looked away as if ashamed.

But she kept going.

It wasn't until her third week that she met Professor Sharma.

He was guest-lecturing on sustainable resource management. Anahita arrived early and sat near the front. The moment he began to speak, something shifted. His voice carried conviction—he spoke of rivers not just as waterways but as lifelines; of soil not as dirt, but memory.

After class, she approached him nervously. "Sir," she said, her voice hesitant, "do you believe nature can still forgive us?"

He studied her for a moment. "Are you asking for nature's forgiveness... or your own?"

"I'm asking for both," she replied honestly.

He smiled. "Then come see me. I think you might belong in my lab."

That was how she began working under Professor Sharma—sorting soil samples, analyzing water data, assisting in community outreach programs. He became a quiet pillar in her new life. He saw beyond her scar, beyond her silence. He saw her.

A week later, in the university garden, she met Rohan.

She was sketching a composting design when he plopped down beside her, munching on a samosa. "That looks like a poop machine," he said with a grin.

She blinked. Then—surprisingly—laughed.

"I mean that in the best way," he added quickly, wiping crumbs from his hoodie. "It's genius. I'm Rohan. You must be new."

She nodded. "Anahita."

He didn't stare at her scar. He asked where she was from. When she said "a village in the Himalayas," his eyes lit up. "No way. I grew up in Chennai. Moved here for the tech program. Bet your place had actual trees, huh?"

They talked for hours that evening. He showed her how to navigate the university portal, introduced her to cheap food stalls, even helped fix her broken laptop with a borrowed screwdriver and a whole lot of patience. His humor was disarming. His loyalty even more so.

Life in the city didn't suddenly become easy. But it became bearable.

The city was a jungle, yes—but amidst its noise and chaos, Anahita began to grow roots of her own. Invisible ones. Ones that clung to values, to memory, to a dream she still carried deep within her: that she had not come to the city to escape her past, but to amplify its message.

She was no longer just the girl from the mountain.

She was becoming something new.

CHAPTER V

Awakening

The campus buzzed with life as spring edged its way into the city. Trees, confined to square soil beds between walkways, struggled into bloom. Students sprawled across the quad with their books and phones, the air filled with chatter, caffeine, and dreams.

But Anahita walked through it all like a river cutting through stone—quiet, deliberate, unbothered by the noise. Her mornings began before dawn. She would light a single stick of incense by the window, breathe deeply, and recite a mantra her mother had taught her to quiet her nerves. Then came the library, the laboratory, the fieldwork.

Under Professor Sharma's guidance, Anahita's world began to expand. He introduced her to journals on ecological restoration, case studies on sustainable architecture, and grassroots environmental movements that had sparked global change. It wasn't just academic—it was personal. She felt the weight of the earth in every word she read, the urgency in every statistic about disappearing forests, poisoned rivers, rising oceans.

Her passion ignited.

She spent hours analyzing soil acidity in urban plots, testing the potential of local weeds to absorb toxins from polluted waterways. Her fingers, once used to peeling bark in the forest, now hovered over microscopes and data sheets. She didn't just study sustainability. She lived it. She recycled obsessively, saved food scraps for compost, and once gave an impromptu lecture in the canteen on single-use plastic that left half the students too guilty to use straws again.

And yet, beneath the surface of this driven purpose, she still wrestled with feeling out of place.

Her accent made her stand out. So did her handmade clothes. And always, the scar.

Until Arjun came along.

He was a senior in the Environmental Engineering department. Charismatic, articulate, and confident in a way that made people lean in when he spoke. Anahita first met him during a student-led seminar on green infrastructure. He complimented her research question during the Q&A—something no one else had done.

Afterward, he invited her for coffee. She was hesitant at first, but his kindness was warm, not pushy. Over time, they began to meet regularly—discussing projects, attending climate rallies, debating policy and tradition.

He made her feel visible. Beautiful, even.

One evening, they sat on the campus terrace under a dusky sky, books forgotten between them.

"You see the world differently," Arjun said, tracing a fingertip along the edge of his mug. "Most people think change starts with big institutions. You believe it starts with soil."

She smiled. "Everything starts with soil. Even revolutions."

He laughed, and for a moment, Anahita allowed herself to imagine a life where this feeling—of being understood, admired—was more than fleeting.

They began collaborating on a research paper: Decentralized Solutions for Urban Sustainability. Anahita poured herself into the project—late nights, endless revisions, careful citations. It was her most ambitious work to date. When they submitted it to a national innovation conference, she felt a tremor of hope.

But hope, she would learn, can be a cruel currency.

Two weeks later, while scrolling through the university's news portal, she froze. There, under the list of accepted papers, was the title of their project. But only Arjun's name was listed.

No mention of her.

She re-read the entry, numb. There had to be a mistake.

She found him later that day, chatting with friends outside the seminar hall. "Arjun," she said quietly, "the conference listing—my name—"

He looked at her for a moment too long. "Oh. Yeah. About that." He lowered his voice. "The organizers only wanted one author. I thought... it might be better if it came from someone more... recognized."

Her breath caught. "Recognized?"

"I mean, you're brilliant, obviously. But I've got the connections. I can get the message out there. That's the point, right?"

She stared at him, her chest hollowing. "You used me."

He flinched. "Don't be dramatic. It's not like that. You'll get credit later."

But she knew. In that moment, with the scar on her cheek burning as if freshly etched, she knew. Her trust had been a gift he'd unwrapped and discarded like paper.

She didn't argue. She simply walked away—each step feeling like the snapping of threads she hadn't realized were binding her.

That night, she didn't cry. She sat at her desk, stared at her notebooks filled with diagrams and dreams, and let silence settle around her. Betrayal didn't shatter her—it clarified her.

The next morning, she went straight to Professor Sharma. She told him everything.

He listened without interrupting, then handed her a copy of Silent Spring by Rachel Carson.

"This book changed the world," he said. "It wasn't written by someone with power. It was written by someone with purpose."

Anahita opened the first page. Something shifted.

She began working on her own research again—this time, on eco-products derived from native plants. She remembered the wildflowers of Sitang, the balm from wild ginger, the lather from soap nuts. She experimented with formulas, tested textures, coded her own ingredients chart.

Her hands, once calloused from digging in Himalayan soil, now blended oils and herbs with the precision of science and the soul of tradition.

Something beautiful was being born—not in a lab, or a relationship, but within her.

It was not the end of heartbreak.

It was the beginning of something stronger: purpose, rooted deep.

CHAPTER VI

Blossoming Venture

The scent of lavender and wild basil now lingered in Anahita's room—not the artificial kind bottled in plastic, but the earthy, honest fragrance of plants drying on cotton sheets, the memory of forests reborn in glass jars. Her desk, once cluttered with academic notes, had become a laboratory of its own—filled with copper bowls, mortar and pestles, tiny labeled containers, and sketches of soap molds and packaging designs.

She had spent weeks experimenting, drawing from memories of her mother's healing blends, from recipes whispered in Sitang's mountain winds. Neem for its antiseptic power, turmeric for glow, rose petals to soften, and coconut husk for texture. She worked with intention, always guided by one question: How can I heal the world without harming it more?

It started small. A simple line of handmade soaps, each wrapped in recycled brown paper and tied with twine. No plastic. No chemicals. Only plants, soil, memory—and hope.

She named the brand EarthKind.

With Rohan's help, she built a modest website. He coded into the night, tweaking every color, every font, until it matched her vision. "Your story should breathe through the screen," he said. "Let them feel your roots."

Anahita was skeptical anyone would buy them. "Why would people choose this," she asked, holding a bar of soap like it was too fragile to matter, "when they have store shelves filled with flashy things?"

Rohan simply shrugged. "Because some people still care."

She launched EarthKind at the university flea market. She had a small wooden table, a borrowed chalkboard sign, and a basket of samples. For hours, people walked by without stopping. Some wrinkled their noses. Others took a flyer, glanced at her scar, and walked on.

Then came a girl named Tanvi.

She picked up a rose-mint soap and held it to her nose. "This smells like my grandmother's garden," she whispered, eyes wide. "You made this?"

Anahita nodded, nervous. "From scratch. No parabens. No plastic."

Tanvi smiled. "I'll take three."

That was the first spark. The next came from a blogger who stumbled across her table and posted a photo captioned, "The forest came to campus." Orders trickled in. A local boutique asked for a trial batch. Her evenings became longer, her fingers stained with turmeric and lavender oil, but her heart lightened with each order that went out.

Still, challenges rose like weeds.

Sourcing sustainable ingredients at scale wasn't easy. Suppliers quoted prices that made her wince. Some didn't understand why she refused plastic packaging. Others promised organic but delivered otherwise. Shipping was expensive. University assignments piled up. Rohan, though tireless, was nearing graduation and had his own battles to fight.

And yet, Anahita persisted.

She refused to compromise.

She woke up earlier. Spoke to farmers outside the city. Learned about permaculture, carbon-neutral shipping, and zero-waste design. Every setback became a new lesson in resilience. When a supplier failed to deliver, she biked two hours to a village to find alternatives. When orders were delayed, she wrote handwritten apologies, slipping extra samples in each package.

"I'm not building a business," she told Professor Sharma one evening. "I'm planting an idea."

He smiled. "And the best ideas grow quietly at first. Like seeds in snow."

Slowly, she began to hire help—other students who struggled to make ends meet, especially those often overlooked. There was

Saira, an economics major who packed products with clinical precision. Jamal, who handled customer queries and told stories behind each ingredient in lyrical prose. Mira, a shy artist who painted beautiful leaf motifs on boxes.

Together, they turned a dream into movement.

And the city began to notice.

A local newspaper ran a feature titled, "The Girl Who Brought the Mountains to Market." Photos showed Anahita in her workshop, smiling beneath string lights, herbs hanging above her like blessings. Her scar, unedited and proud, was there for all to see.

It became a symbol—not of what she had suffered, but of what she had overcome.

Customers began sending her letters. "My skin has never felt better." "This reminds me of home." "You gave me a reason to believe people still care."

One letter stood out:

"My daughter has facial scars too. She saw your photo and said, 'She looks like me. And she's amazing.'"

Anahita wept when she read it.

Not because she had succeeded.

But because she realized why she had started.

She was no longer just healing skin.

She was healing something deeper—in herself, in others, in the cracked earth beneath their feet.

As the monsoon approached, rain painted the city with new life. On a rooftop garden above the workshop, she planted the seed Devi had given her. It sprouted slowly, its green no brighter than the rest—but to Anahita, it was sacred. A reminder of roots, of rivers, of a mother's faith.

And with it, EarthKind bloomed—not just as a brand, but a promise.

CHAPTER VII

Shadows of Greed

The workshop buzzed with the scent of lemon balm and beeswax. Anahita stood barefoot on the cool tiled floor, sleeves rolled to her elbows, blending a new batch of herbal body butters. The scent of earth and rain clung to her skin like a memory. In one corner, Rohan adjusted the new POS system. Mira painted batch numbers onto glass jars. The team laughed between orders, their hands busy, their hearts light.

EarthKind was no longer a hopeful whisper. It had become a voice.

Sales doubled within six months. The online store, once a simple scroll of product photos and hand-typed descriptions, was now a curated digital experience, showcasing not just goods, but stories—of farmers, of forest rituals, of the science behind each formula. Urban wellness bloggers praised her ethics. Environmentalists quoted her in talks. Young entrepreneurs wrote asking how she had started with nothing but herbs, a scar, and a mission.

It wasn't about fame. Anahita still walked to the workshop every day. Still touched every batch before it was packed. Still insisted on writing thank-you notes in her crooked, careful script. But success brought attention—and not all of it kind.

The first letter came in a sleek white envelope with no return address. Inside, a gold-embossed business card and a typed note:

"Ms. Anahita,

You have built something impressive. Let us help you grow it. Our investors are interested in scaling your brand to a national—and international—level. Let's discuss terms.

—Marcus Thorne

CEO, Thorne Biocorp"

Rohan frowned when he read it. "Thorne Biocorp? They're notorious. Pesticide lobbyists. Known for bulldozing tribal lands for their so-called green farms."

"I've heard of them," Anahita said, voice low. "They sell sustainability the way fast-food chains sell happiness."

"But they've got power," Rohan said. "If they're reaching out, it means you've rattled the right cages."

Anahita tucked the letter into a drawer. "I'm not for sale."

The next email was more aggressive. Promises of warehouses, marketing campaigns, television slots. A blank cheque for acquisition. When she refused, the tone shifted.

First came the rumors—planted on social media, whispered in business forums. Claims that EarthKind used exploitative labor. That her certifications were forged. That her products caused rashes. An anonymous blog posted an "exposé" on her scar, implying it had been fabricated for pity marketing.

"I've handled stares my whole life," Anahita said, jaw clenched. "But now they're trying to use my pain as a weapon."

She wanted to stay silent. Focus on the work. But silence, she realized, was fertile ground for lies.

So she spoke.

She released a public statement—calm, measured, factual. She opened her doors to journalists. Invited customers into her workshop. Published a transparency report with sourcing details, labor wages, environmental impact metrics. Her employees, suppliers, and customers rallied. Videos of her team packing orders, singing folk songs, laughing over herbal teas went viral.

But Thorne wasn't done.

Next came legal letters—claims that her packaging resembled theirs, that her "soil-safe" formula infringed on a patent they conveniently registered just months ago. Her inbox became a battlefield. Her staff, once relaxed and playful, worked with tightened brows and quiet mouths.

Sales dropped.

One afternoon, Anahita stood in her garden, staring at the seedling she had planted long ago. Its leaves were curled from too much sun. A metaphor, she thought. Even things rooted in care could wilt under greed.

That night, she returned to the river.

Not the one from Sitang—but the river that slithered through the city like a wounded snake. Its waters reeked of chemicals, its banks littered with forgotten things. She sat by its edge, closed her eyes, and listened—not to the noise, but to the pulse beneath it.

"I didn't come this far," she whispered, "to sell out what brought me here."

The next morning, she called her team. "They want us to stop growing," she said. "So let's grow smarter."

They began sourcing from more independent farmers. Launched a campaign called Rooted Real, inviting people to share stories of scars that had made them stronger. Anahita spoke at schools, panels, town halls—teaching not just sustainability, but courage.

Then, she did something bold.

She published a dossier—compiled by volunteers, activists, and citizen researchers—documenting Thorne Biocorp's violations: chemical leaks, farmer suicides, illegal land grabs, silencing of whistleblowers. She cited everything. Dates. Names. Photos.

It spread like wildfire.

Investigations followed. News outlets picked it up. Former employees came forward. One headline read:

"The Girl with the Scar vs. The Corporate Machine: Anahita's Battle for EarthKind Justice."

But Anahita didn't want war.

She wanted change.

"Let them burn their name," she said. "We'll plant ours."

EarthKind didn't just survive. It evolved. Stores that once hesitated began to reach out. Students campaigned to stock her products in eco-friendly campuses. Her team expanded, trained new hires from underserved communities. They implemented vertical gardens in slums. Held workshops in villages. Reinvested profits into building local cooperatives.

Marcus Thorne sent one final message: "**You've made powerful enemies.**"

Anahita replied with three words: "**I make powerful roots.**"

23

CHAPTER VIII

Voice of Change

The city had begun to echo her name—not in admiration alone, but in defiance. In classrooms, at street corners, in quiet homes with soil-filled window boxes, the story of EarthKind was whispered, shared, sung. Not just the products, but the woman behind them: the scarred girl from the mountains who stood against an empire.

Anahita never set out to be a symbol. But the world was starving for someone who believed in healing more than profit.

Her days grew longer, her nights shorter. She no longer worked just in a workshop—she was in boardrooms, on panels, in village meetings, video calls with environmental councils, podcasts, and interviews. She traveled to schools across the country, planting trees with students and speaking to them in the same tone Devi had once used with her—gentle but unyielding.

"The earth doesn't need pity," she told a group of children sitting cross-legged in a dusty schoolyard. "It needs protectors."

Professor Sharma watched her from afar with pride. Rohan, now working full-time with her as head of strategy, often joked, "I signed up for herbal soap. Ended up in a revolution."

But it was far from easy.

Thorne Biocorp, though shaken, hadn't gone quietly. Their influence reached deep into corridors of power. Politicians who once smiled at Anahita's photo-ops now avoided her calls. Legal pressure mounted. Inspections became frequent. Grants she had previously qualified for were mysteriously denied.

Then came the threats.

Emails filled with veiled warnings. Packages arriving with dead leaves and anonymous notes: "Some weeds need to be pulled before they spread."

She began traveling with a volunteer security team. Her staff received training on digital safety. Her parents in Sitang were offered relocation, but Devi declined.

"If they think fear will uproot you," she said calmly over a video call, "remind them you were raised by the mountains."

But the strain was real.

Anahita grew thinner. Her sleep became fractured. Rohan noticed the way her shoulders stiffened whenever the doorbell rang, how she flinched at sudden noises. Still, she refused to retreat.

She began organizing Green Assemblies—public gatherings where people shared local eco-solutions, exchanged seeds, traded products, and told stories of resistance. These weren't just awareness campaigns. They were acts of reclamation. Children planted trees in plastic-polluted lots. Elders taught composting. Musicians sang in folk languages of the rivers their grandparents had loved.

Anahita stood in the center of these circles, not as a leader, but as a listener.

In one such event, an eleven-year-old girl with vitiligo stood beside her and said, "Everyone told me I had spots. You told me I had stars."

The audience wept. So did Anahita.

Meanwhile, her expose on Thorne Biocorp continued to gain traction. Independent journalists unearthed deeper layers—offshore accounts, shell companies, and forged sustainability certifications. A whistleblower, a former Thorne scientist, reached out. With their testimony, Anahita filed a civil suit backed by a coalition of green entrepreneurs.

The trial was long and grueling. She was cross-examined for hours. They questioned her credentials, her upbringing, even her scar—suggesting it was leveraged for sympathy. The room fell silent when she stood, walked to the bench, and simply said:

"This scar saved my life. It reminds me of what I survived—and why I'll never let others suffer in silence."

The courtroom broke into applause.

In the end, the verdict wasn't complete victory—but it was enough. Thorne Biocorp was ordered to pay fines, withdraw products, and publicly apologize. More importantly, their name was tarnished in the public eye. Shareholders pulled support. Partnerships crumbled.

Anahita declined interviews that wanted to paint her as "the girl who brought down a giant."

"I didn't bring them down," she said. "I held up a mirror. They fell on their own."

Her voice was no longer hers alone. It belonged to every young girl with a dream buried under doubt. Every community that had been told they were too small to matter. Every seed that had once been stepped on, and now pushed back through the cracks in concrete.

And so she kept speaking.

At climate conferences, where delegates quoted her alongside global figures.

In slums, where she helped launch community gardens and rooftop solar grids.

In parliament halls, where she submitted green policy drafts written not by lobbyists, but by farmers and teachers.

She was offered awards. Some she accepted with grace. Others she declined, asking for funds to be redirected to grassroots groups.

Her face, once dismissed, now graced magazine covers with headlines like:

"The Future is EarthKind."

"Anahita: Scarred, Sacred, Unstoppable."

"From Soil to Speaker: One Woman's Fight for a Kinder Planet."

But she never forgot the girl who had once stared into a mirror and asked why the river had marked her.

Now she knew.

It hadn't marked her.

It had chosen her.

CHAPTER IX

Legacy of Hope

The sun rose slowly over the city, casting golden light across rooftops, softening the harsh angles of glass and steel. On one of those rooftops stood a garden—lush, wild, defiant. In its center, Anahita knelt by a blooming Himalayan blue poppy. She touched its fragile petals with reverence. This flower, grown from the seed her mother had once pressed into her hand, had survived two harsh winters. Just like her.

She rose, wiped her hands on her kurta, and looked out at the cityscape. There were fewer trees than she wished for, too much noise, too much haste—but here and there, she saw the ripples of change. A terrace with compost bins. A park with restored wetlands. A school with solar panels. It wasn't a revolution. It was a return.

She had spent years planting seeds in the cracks of broken systems. Now, some of those seeds were blooming.

Her days were filled with new rhythms. No longer just a founder or activist, Anahita was now a mentor, a guide. Young people came to her in waves—students, dreamers, quiet visionaries—each carrying ideas nurtured in shadows. They brought their doubts, their inventions, their pain.

She welcomed them all.

"I don't want to be anyone's hero," she often told them. "I want to be your bridge. So you can cross and build something better on the other side."

She established the EarthKind Foundation, a nonprofit arm focused on empowering underprivileged youth through environmental education, skill-building, and micro-grants. The first campus was built on the edge of the city, on land that had once been a dumping ground. Volunteers cleaned it, transformed it with gardens, greenhouses, and solar classrooms. Children from slums and villages now sat on benches made of recycled wood, learning from teachers who spoke their language, both literally and metaphorically.

She named the campus Prakriti Mandir—Temple of Nature.

The Foundation's work expanded quickly. From waste management programs in remote towns to herbal healthcare clinics in tribal areas. Anahita traveled extensively—not as a celebrity, but as a listener. She sat cross-legged in dusty courtyards, under banyan trees, beside wells, in railway schools, always with a notepad and an open heart.

"Don't build towers," she told her teams. "Build roots. We're not here to extract—we're here to grow."

Still, despite the momentum, there were days when she grew tired. Her body had borne the cost of years spent pushing against mountains. Old aches returned. Sleepless nights deepened the lines on her face. The scar remained, but now it was part of something larger—a map etched by fire, water, and will.

One summer, she returned to Sitang.

The air smelled the same—pine and prayer. Children ran barefoot through the same trails she once followed, and the river hummed a familiar tune.

Devi, now older but no less radiant, stood waiting at the village gate. They embraced silently, tears forming where words failed.

"You came back," Devi whispered, her voice breaking.

"I never left," Anahita replied, touching the amulet still hanging around her neck.

She spent days walking old paths, speaking to villagers, planting fruit trees near the school. The people gathered to honor her with a simple ceremony—flowers, songs, a clay plaque in her name.

But Anahita refused to stand on a stage.

She chose instead to kneel with the children and plant the first sapling for a new community nursery. "Let this be your forest," she told them. "Guard it better than we ever did."

Devi later sat beside her, watching the sun set behind the snow-streaked peaks.

"I'm proud of you, Anu," she said, brushing hair from her daughter's brow. "Not because of the awards or buildings. But because you remembered who you were, even when the world tried to forget."

Anahita smiled, leaning into her mother's shoulder.

Back in the city, she launched the Green Seed Scholarship—a program that provided full academic sponsorship to rural students pursuing environmental sciences. Each recipient received not just funding, but mentorship, internships, and a plot of land to cultivate their own project. The program became a model replicated in countries across Asia and Africa.

The girl who once thought her scar made her different had become the reason others dared to be themselves.

At a major global sustainability summit, Anahita received a lifetime achievement award. She stood before a sea of dignitaries, her voice steady.

"I didn't grow up with machines or degrees or wealth. I grew up with soil under my nails, and stories whispered into leaves. That was enough. More than enough. We don't need to invent new worlds. We need to remember the one we already had."

The applause rose like thunder. But her heart remained quiet.

Because she knew—her work wasn't the legacy.

The people were.

The girl in Meghalaya designing bamboo air purifiers.

The boy in Rajasthan building clay water coolers for villages.

The child in a slum who wrote a poem about trees and signed it Inspired by Anahita.

These were her echoes.

And they were only just beginning.

The river was gentle that morning, as if it, too, understood the passage of time.

Anahita sat by its bank, wrapped in a soft shawl woven by village women she had mentored years ago. The same waters that once kissed her cheeks as a child now flowed past her wrinkled hands. Her bones ached, her hair had long turned silver, and her body had grown thin—but her eyes, those stormy Himalayan eyes, were still alight with life.

She had returned to Sitang for what she quietly knew would be the final time.

The illness had come silently, as it had once before. Not a fever this time, but something deeper—an invisible fraying of the thread that bound her to this earth. Her doctors in the city had been gentle but honest. Her body, worn by years of movement and purpose, was growing tired.

But she wasn't afraid.

She had always known life was a river. It flowed, it carved, it carried. Now, it was simply time to let it carry her home.

In the village, the people walked with reverence around her—not in mourning, but in quiet celebration. Children brought her flowers, elders asked for her blessing, and the trees seemed to lean in just a little closer as she passed.

Every day, she sat by the river, dictating notes, voice-recording final ideas, reviewing proposals for projects she would never see but still wanted to plant. Her team in the city stayed connected. Rohan visited often, now older and greyer himself, his laugh as loud and loving as ever.

"You should rest," he told her, kneeling beside her one evening.

She smiled. "This is rest. Sitting by the river. Letting things be."

Professor Sharma, retired but still sharp-eyed, came to see her, too. They sat in silence most of the visit, watching the wind stir the water.

"You changed more than the world, Anahita," he said as he left. "You changed what people believe is possible."

She didn't respond. She only touched his hand and nodded, eyes full.

On her last morning, she asked to be brought to the highest hill above the village—the place she once sat as a girl, wondering what lay beyond the peaks.

Devi, now bent with age but still bright in spirit, sat beside her.

"You remember," Anahita whispered, "when I said I wanted to go beyond the mountains?"

Devi smiled through tears. "I do. And you did. But the mountain never left you."

They sat there, mother and daughter, heart and soil, until the sun began to dip below the peaks.

That night, Anahita fell asleep under the stars, wrapped in a quilt of memories. And in the early hours, as the river began its soft hymn and the village held its breath, she slipped away—like mist into sky, like a seed into earth, like a dream into eternity.

But her story did not end.

The EarthKind Foundation flourished. The Green Seed Scholarship doubled its reach. The rooftop gardens she helped build grew into city forests. Her teachings were adapted into textbooks. Her name was whispered with reverence—not as a saint or a savior, but as a reminder.

On the first anniversary of her passing, children from across the country gathered in Sitang. They brought saplings—teak, neem, bamboo, flowering gulmohar—and planted them in a wide clearing along the river. They sang songs she had once written, recited poems she had loved, and etched her name into smooth stones placed beneath the trees.

At the center of it all, a plaque stood tall:

"Here lies the spirit of Anahita—daughter of rivers, mother of dreams.

She flowed not to escape the mountain, but to return to it with rain."

The wind carried their laughter. The earth cradled their roots. The river flowed on.

And in every leaf that danced, in every child who dared to believe, in every scar worn with pride, her echo lived on—

Soft. Strong. Eternal.

www.ingramcontent.com/pod-product-compliance
Lightning Source LLC
Chambersburg PA
CBHW021149130726
47988CB00004B/1530